TERRY THE TOMBOY A.K.A. LOVESDIRT96, HERE AGA

Hey there, selfie takers and memory makers! Terry the Tomboy, a.k.a. Lovesdirt96, here again! And I'm happier than a tornado in a trailer park, ready to unveil this here scrapbook of my life that I've been working on for the past couple of years!

You're gonna lo-o-o-ve it!

It's plumb full of my best photos, all crammed together in one place for maximum viewing pleasure! That's right media darlin's, it's (cue play my theme music in your head) my "Terry The Tomboy's This Here's My Awesome Life, Y'all!" scrapbook!

TERRY THE TOMBOY
A.K.A. LOVESDIRT96

THIS HERE'S MY AWESOME LIFE, Y'ALL!

MEET THE PEOPLE IN MY LIFE

(EVEN MY ARCH NEMESIS BRITANNICA,

WHO USED TO BE MY BFF)!

This wouldn't be a scrapbook without some scraps
about my friends and family now would it?
So without further ado
(cue that theme music in your head again, please!), this here's
"Meet The People In My Life (Even My Arch Nemesis
Britannica Who Used To Be My BFF)!"

FIRST, ME

My name's Terry Ptarmigan. I'm a tomboy. You can tell I'm a tomboy on account a' my clothes. And also on account a' I just told you.

I like forest animals. And cooking. And sometimes cooking forest animals. (But only the nasty ones who are not my friends, and who are not friends of my other forest animal friends.) I also like cooking with forest animals—especially squirrels, chipmunks, prairie dogs, and other furry, four-legged members of the Sciuridae species—who really know how to make great pizza.

You can probably tell I grew up in the forest. (I practically did.) My fondest memories are of frolicking in the woods with a lizard and a squirrel. (I'm talking about you, Razzle and Beauregard!)

Currently, I live in a house and I go to high school. When I'm not there, I can usually be found here in my work shed, a.k.a. my garage, where I'm busier than a tick on a kitty cat's back, making an awesome vlog for my millions upon millions upon millions of fans.

(Okay, maybe I'm exaggerating a little there, but my blog does get a lot of hits.)

DUNCANTY

Now, it may seem like I only keep Duncanty around so I'll have someone to mess with all the time—and he is a darn-good victim—but if we're being honest here, and I pride myself in being honest as much as possible, Duncanty is also a darn-good sport and my best friend, hands down.

Sometimes, even hands up—as you can see.

KERRY

I met my BTFF (Best Tomboy Friend Forever) Kerry when she first moved into town and into my school. Now, see, I was already gunnin' for the title of "Most Favorite Tomboy" at school. But from her very first "Wassup?" it was clear Kerry was bent on dethroning me. Then a lot of other stuff happened, which you can see for yourself later on in this scrapbook, and now, I'm happy to report, we're best friends!

REESE

Just because I tricked Reese into asking me to prom with a rebus, doesn't mean we didn't have an amazing time!

And by "amazing," I mean "awkward."

Luckily, he was able to get past my homemade prom dress, and the fact that I strapped a boom box to my back for our "grand entrance" and we're still great friends anyway! I even once heard him refer to our date as "that time I went to prom with Terry and was chagrined beyond humanly possible." Awesome, right? (I'm not entirely sure what *chagrined* means, but it has the word *grin* in it, so it must be good.)

MADISON (MADDY)

Maddy and I became friends when she came to my house desperate for a makeover. And I agreed—she was totally lacking any sense of style! I mean, her hair was long and wavy and perfectly done up (gross!), her clothes were pretty and elegant and ironed, and—this here's the worst part—she was wearing make-up! *shudder*

Thank heavens I got to her when I did.

Here's a picture of Maddy after I worked my magic! (You can see other pictures from that day on pages 32 and 33: My Makeover!)

BRITANNICA

We used to be best friends, and now we're not even frenemies! We are archenemies, ever since the time she discovered makeup on the roof of my house and ruined the primo stunt we were about to pull. I won't go into detail (especially about the stunt, which made my ma madder than a box of frogs! Sorry, Ma), but I *will* say: "You're pretty much dead to me, Britannica!" Also, "You smell like potatoes!"

MY CHILDHOOD FRIENDS

Growin' up in the forest wasn't easy. But, luckily, making friends there was! We didn't have cell phone selfies back then, or even cell phones, so I drew you a picture of my BFFs (Best Forest Friends). Ever since I moved out of the forest and into a (*yuck!*) house, I miss them somethin' awful. :(

This here's Beatrice the rabbit, Razzle the lizard, Beauregard the squirrel, and Ronald the badger—the best security guard that ever lived.

MY FAMILY

(Oh, right . . . my family.)

So there's my **mom**, who's great and all, but she's always grumpy, and she's always wanted me to be a ballerina and wear pink stuff.

That's about it. I mean the pink thing can be pretty annoying, so I try not to have long, deep conversations with her (unless we're cuttin' down trees or drainin' the sink together). Ma's camera shy, so I had to draw you her portrait, too.

Then there's my **younger brother Brian**, who always wanted to be a ballerina, but settles for being on the cheer squad at school. He can be cool once in a while, but for the most part, he's pretty irritating. I drew his picture, too—not because he's camera shy, but because I don't have any photos of him that don't irritate me.

Finally, there's my **other brother Tim, a.k.a. Tim Who Knows Nothin' About Bacon**. He's not my real brother—he's my blood brother, which, in my opinion, is even better. Tim Who Knows Nothin' About Bacon and I have been friends ever since we were little and made a blood pact with a rusty can lid. Once he got out of the hospital from the botulism he got from the rusty can lid, we were inseparable!

Tim Who Knows Nothin' About Bacon and I have loads of fun paintin' and goofin' around together, but the thing we most like to do is argue over whether or not we argue. (We don't.) (Zip it, Tim Who Knows Nothin' About Bacon! We don't!)

THIS HERE'S MY ROOM TOUR!

Welcome to my room. Come on now, I'll give you the grand tour!

Sure, I have a dresser. But unlike regular people who keep their clothes in their dresser, I prefer to utilize my floor space for clothes and keep more important things in my dresser drawers.

I remember this like it was yesterday! The day I found my pet bat Rascal! I'd plumb forgot he was even in that dresser drawer there! When I found him, boy was he thirsty. I gotta keep my eye on Rascal from now on 'cuz he has a habit of…of… wait, where'd he go? Come to think of it, I haven't seen him since I took this picture. Rascal? Where the heck are you?

Here's some vital Terry the Tomboy advice: You should keep your leaf blower in your room at all times! It's perfect for when your mom says, "Clean your room!"

Most of you guys probably keep your hairbrush and other tools for grooming in the drawer of your vanity table. Not me! Call me Miss Practicality because I use my vanity table drawer for more important necessities—namely, my fine meats and cheeses!

If you're the type who gets jealous, get ready to be greener than a frog in a meadow when you see my collection of stuffed animals! Pretty amazing, right?

What's that?

Well of course I stuffed 'em myself! Sheesh! Who stuffs your animals?

Now this part of my room tour is top secret, everyone. Can I trust you to keep your lips zipped? I don't want my brother Brian to find out about the stuff I've got stashed away under my bed. Especially my box of rocks. Or my box of teeth. Or my box of rocks that look like teeth. Brian's such a neat freak, he'd think it was junk and throw it out! Just like he did with my box of junk. And I was savin' that for Christmas!

NO TRESPASSING

MY FAVORITE THINGS (IN NO PARTICULAR ORDER)

Y'all already know how much I love dirt (lovesdirt96, duh), but how many of you tomboy compatriots know what else makes me happier 'n a june bug on a tomato plant? If you don't know, lucky for you, you can refer to this here handy-dandy list of:

My Favorite Things (In No Particular Order)

MY M-15 ISRAELI GAS MASK FROM THE ARMY/NAVY SURPLUS

Sure, the GP5 Russian gas mask and filter was a lot cheaper, but when it comes to my dad on chili night, I wasn't taken' any chances!

MY POTATO CHIP COLLECTION

From my most-prized chip—the one that looks like Abraham Lincoln—to my other most-prized chip—the one of my Uncle Gray-ham, which Duncanty ATE by accident and which made me want to beat him even more senseless than he already is—my potato chip collection makes me giddier then my fat Uncle Gray-ham at an all-you-can-eat buffet!

MY HOT DOG HAT

No explanation needed. (How awesome is this hat?)

MY FAVORITE BOOK: FIVE MINUTE RUFFING, THE SAGA OF A HOCKEY DOG

Any book with a dog or a wolf as the protagonist is a good book in my book!

ANIMAL TRAP WARS, THE TV SHOW I MADE MYSELF!

A bidding war for the mystery contents of an animal trap? Now why haven't the TV people gotten on-board with my brilliant idea for a show? Sheesh! Seems like a no-brainer, if you ask me.

ANY SPANISH SOAP OPERA

Other than *Animal Trap Wars*, my favorite TV show is any Spanish soap opera.

BEAVERS

My favorite animal, paws down. Do you really need me to explain why? Isn't it enough that their teeth are sharp enough to rip through tree bark? Precious is what they are, really.

PIZZA SHAKES

I couldn't choose which I liked more—pizza or milkshakes—so I combined the two! It's real simple to make: just take some pizza and some ice cream, put 'em both in the blender for 30 seconds, and there ya go!

Not a fan of pizza shakes? (Are you one of those people with a pizza intolerance?) No reason you can't have a regular milkshake. If pizza shakes just aren't your thing, try one of these "My Ma Approved Them" milkshakes.

The Peanut Butter Milkshake: 1 pint of vanilla ice cream, 1–1/2 cups of whole milk, 1/4 cup of creamy peanut butter, and 1 teaspoon of vanilla extract. Place the ingredients in a blender, and blend. (Don't overmix if you like a thicker milkshake.) Serve immediately.

Banana Milkshake: 1 pint of vanilla ice cream, 1 very ripe banana, 1 cup of whole milk, 1/2 teaspoon of vanilla extract. Same directions as above.

A TAG WITH YOURS TRULY!

You've got some random questions for me, and I've got some random answers!

Q: What have you never eaten before?

TERRY: I have never in my life eaten a snow pea.

Q: What do you want to be when you grow up?

TERRY: A landscaper. Because beavers are my favorite animal and they are called "nature's landscapers."

Q: Do you play sports in school?

TERRY: I got kicked off my soccer team once because I got distracted trying to save a praying mantis that had wandered onto the field.

Q: What are you afraid of?

TERRY: Trains. I know it's irrational, but trains scare the bejeezus out of me.

Q: What do you do when you're bored?

TERRY: I draw cuboids.

Q: What is your favorite word?

TERRY: Bubble.

Q: Name something you dislike.

TERRY: I can't stand the smell of peaches. (Or potatoes. Or Britannica, 'cuz she smells like potatoes!)

Q: What do you dream about at night?

TERRY: I have the same dream every night—that I'm a bug zapper.

Q: What is something nobody knows about you?

TERRY: My eyelids squeak when I blink too hard.

Q: How many selfies do you take a day?

TERRY: Oh, I love selfies! I probably take ten a day!

THAT TIME WHEN . . .

Boy, I sure have some wonderful memories from my life! Happy, carefree times. I remember them like they were yesterday...some of 'em even were from yesterday...

This photo brings back so many memories, it just warms my heart! Remember that time I played a little joke on Duncanty? "Have a nice trip! See ya next fall..."

A-HAHAHAHAHAHAHAH!

(Gets me every time.)

Oh, and that time I got Duncanty real good with a bucket of hot sauce! I nearly busted a gut that day! I mean, who walks into a room on April Fool's Day without looking up first anyway??? I swear, sometimes that boy is nine dimes short of a dollar.

Before you start feelin' sorry for the guy, just remember it was yours truly who helped cool him down after the previously mentioned hot sauce incident! That's right, Terry the Tomboy to the rescue! You're welcome, Duncanty.

All these fond memories...I'm startin' to feel a little misty-eyed! I'm so grateful I could spend all these quality moments with my good buddy Duncanty! I 'specially remember this one time I gave him quite a shock. A "shock," get it?

I'll always treasure my Christmas memories. I even remember all the times I exchanged gifts with my buddy Duncanty. I don't think he wants to remember this one particular Christmas gift exchange, though. I know I don't! After he let my pet squirrel Bentley escape, I put a knot in Ohis noggin he couldn't untie! (Hey, Duncanty, I'm still madder than a long-tailed cat in a room full of rocking chairs!)

This here's a picture of Duncanty and me on New Year's Eve. At first, he didn't want to spend New Year's Eve with me. But then I promised him I wouldn't deck him in the face or pour hot sauce on his head, so he changed his mind. And I kept my promise, just as good friends always do! So if you're wondering why Duncanty has a bloody nose in this photograph, it's because...well...he ended up decking himself in the face that night! Just for laughs, I suppose. Duncanty can be hilarious sometimes, I tell ya!

17

Before y'all say anything or call me a mean girl, or whatever, this was an accident! AND I got detention for it! AND I hurt my hand!

In all seriousness, all's I was tryin' to do was give my buddy Duncanty a high five. I certainly wasn't tryin' to smack him in the face! (Well, not entirely anyway.) So even though this memory may not be a cherished memory, it still happened and I'm still puttin' it in this here scrapbook.

I'd do anything for my pal Duncanty, as you probably know by now. Once I even helped him with his Valentine's Day date! Nothin' a little shot from cupid, a.k.a. Yours Truly, couldn't handle!

Nothing makes me angrier than a dog eatin' peanut butter than when Duncanty doesn't return my texts! Best friend or not, I don't let him get away with it, no siree! A while back, I turbo'd up my fishing rod and made me a super strong line with GPS capabilities! One cast and I captured that little ignoring weasel and reeled him in!

The best time ever? Oh, that's easy. It was the time Duncanty and I got into a little tiff about breakfast cereals.

As you can see, I won that tiff.

Good times!

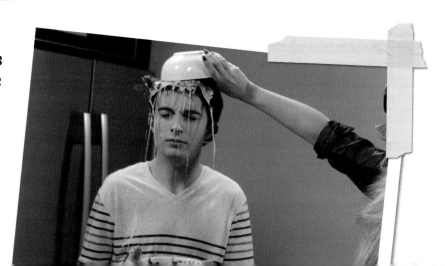

THIS HERE'S MY TOP 10 LIST OF TOP 10 LISTS!

MY TOP 10 LIST OF TOP 10 LISTS:

10. My Top 10 Things In My Schoolbag
9. My Top 10 Things In My Fairly Small Beach Tote Bag
8. My Top 10 Arch Nemeses
7. My Top 10 #TomboyProblems
6. My Top 10 Ridiculous-But-Fun Dances, Some I Made Up Myself!

5. My Top 10 Things I Can Cook
4. My Top 10 Things I Suck At
3. My Top 10 Firsts
2. My Top 10 Uses For Chewed-Up Gum
1. My Top 10 Sayin's, Or, Words A' Wisdom

MY TOP 10 THINGS IN MY SCHOOLBAG

10. Paper
9. Pencils
8. Abacus
7. Bottle rockets
6. Slingshot
5. Chewed gum
4. Favorite roadkill-skinned binder
3. Car battery for teaching bullies a lesson
2. Bucket of water for teaching mean girls a lesson
1. Lunch (See my next chapter on packing a delicious and nutritious school lunch!)

MY TOP 10 THINGS IN MY FAIRLY SMALL BEACH TOTE BAG

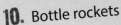

10. Bottle rockets
9. *Of Mice and Men* DVD
8. Creepy owl statue
7. Old time gas lantern
6. Horse mask

5. Gallon of distilled water
4. Boxing gloves
3. Comical scissors
2. 40 latex balloons
1. An iron

MY TOP 10 #TOMBOYPROBLEMS

10. Our moms insist on bedazzling our skateboards.
9. Our barbed-wire bracelets always cut our arms.
8. We mistake our best tomboy friend for a boy.
7. People think we're boys.
6. We can't rub dirt on our problems to make them go away.
5. Sometimes our car battery engages the starter on its own so we disconnect the relay starter side, turn the key on, and then it jumps right from the bait to the starter to the wire, and then it starts and runs so you try a three relay and it does the same thing.

   (I hate when that happens.)

4. We're better than our boyfriends at baseball.
3. We're better than our boyfriends at belching.
2. We're better than our boyfriends at sports.
1. We're better than our boyfriends at everything.

MY TOP 10 ARCH NEMESES

10. Britannica
9. Britannica
8. Britannica
7. Britannica
6. Britannica
5. Britannica
4. Britannica
3. Britannica
2. Britannica
1. BRITANNICA

MY TOP 10 RIDICULOUS-BUT-FUN DANCES, SOME I MADE UP MYSELF

10. The Grenade Pull
9. The Eight-Limbed Man
8. The Insulting Chicken (With Sauce)
7. The Pillow-Fight Prance
6. The Roll in The Mud

5. The Celebration
4. The Football
3. The Untangler
2. The I Got Hot Sauce in My Eye
1. The Thanksgiving Gift of Break Dance

MY TOP 10 THINGS I CAN COOK

10. Momlettes
9. Sweet Potato Pie with French Fries and Honey (and Cheese Puffs, of course)
8. Crushed, Mutilated Pumpkin Pie
7. Tub of Butter Sauce
6. Chili and Chocolate Milk (Not at the same time, silly. Hey, wait, that could work...)
5. Reindeer Jerky (during reindeer season only)
4. Old Man and the Brie Nachos
3. Meatballs in Marinara (but not for eating, for decorating the Christmas tree)
2. Pizza Shakes
1. Road Kill a la King

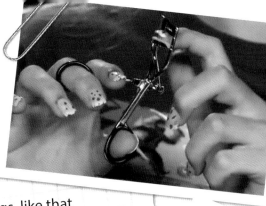

MY TOP 10 THINGS I SUCK AT

10. Brushing my hair

9. Washing my face

8. Putting on sunblock

7. Painting my nails

6. Using this mysterious ancient torturing device

5. Smelling peaches

4. Eating snow peas

3. Using a 55-gallon shop vacuum to dry myself off

2. Remembering things, like that I keep my meats and cheeses in my vanity drawer

1. Getting ready for school in the morning. (It takes me, like, forty or fifty seconds! I really need to shave some time off of that.)

MY TOP 10 FIRSTS

10. First Tweet: the Brown-Headed Cowbird

9. First YouTube: "Say Hello to Mutton the Sheep" on EweTube

8. First Teacher: Miss Barella

7. First Thing I Do In The Morning: Wake up. (Duuuhhh . . .)

6. First Thing I Do When I Get Home: Change into my comfy clothes, of course!

5. First Text: My cell phone is as old as the hills. (I don't text.)

4. First Person I Think About In The Mornng: Mutton the Sheep. *sniff* (RIP, Mutton the Sheep.)

3. First Food: CHILI, of course!

2. First Piece Of Gum: The one I'm chewing right now! I've had it ever since my first tooth came in! I put it on my vanity table every night before I go to sleep.

1. First Toy: My sweet little pocket knife. Every baby should have one!

MY TOP 10 USES FOR CHEWED-UP GUM

10. Hanging pictures.

9. As a reminder.

8. Gettin' a guy's attention. (Spit-straw it to the back of the neck!)

7. Teeth whitening (You need really white gum though.)

6. Art projects: Collect your chewed-up gum and build a gum statue of your brother for his birthday. It's both simple and practical—if he ever runs out of gum, he can just pick one off the statue!

5. Bait. It's a little-known fact that catfish, in particular, love bubble gum. Attach some to your fishing hook and reel in your dinner!

4. School supplies. Works better than staples or paper clips for holding paper together.

3. Bandages. Stop the bleeding fast!

2. Combating boredom. Waiting in line at the auto supply store? Keep a piece behind your ear or on your elbow for fun times while you wait!

1. Dentures. I don't have 'em, but my little cousin does. (He lost all his teeth when he was seven.) I save my chewed-up gum for him for when he needs somethin' to keep his dentures in. Come to think of it, if your grandparents wear dentures, you ought to start saving your gum— makes a nice holiday gift! (You're welcome.)

MY TOP 10 SAYINS', OR WORDS A' WISDOM

10. "A noogie and a loogie and you're ready to boogie!"

9. "A fish fight is better than a fist fight, am I right?"

8. "If at first you don't succeed ... use duct tape!"

7. "Keep your head in the clouds and your feet in the dirt!"

6. "Call me butter, 'cuz I'm on a roll!"

5. "I'm fishin' for koi and jumpin' for joy!"

4. "If you wanna be seen, you gotta stay clean and mean!"

3. "Jiminy Brisket!"

2. "Booty you, Scrooge!"

1. "A little grime is more than fine!"

HOW TO BE A SCHOOL MULE LIKE MYSELF!

Hey there, troublemakers and poor test takers! It's time to memorize and regurgitate facts we'll forget about in a year anyway...

That's right—it's time for SCHOOL! (Cue music agai—nah, never mind. My theme music is too peppy for school.)

Anyway, I like to make a list of things to do in the morning before school. Especially because my memory isn't so great at the ungodly hour I have to be up in order to get to school!

Here's what my list looks like.

1. BREAKFAST

Personally, I like bacon and eggs for breakfast. And luckily, our chicken Wendy provides me with lots of free-range eggs every day. You should make sure your eggs are free range, too. (I'm pretty sure "free range" means they are free of cholesterol.)

2. SHAVE

I know what y'all are thinking: Terry, what could you possibly have to shave? Is this your dad's back-to-school list or somethin'?

But it's true, my friends. Otherwise, I'd go to school looking like this...

3. SHOWER

Hang on just one cottonpickin' minute!!!
"Ma! Stop adding things to my checklist!"
Okay, I'm back. Never mind—scratch number three.

4. HAIR

I'm one of the lucky few who has perfect hair when she wakes up every morning! No brushing or combing needed 'round here!

5. WARDROBE

I'm not one of those kids who feels she has to wear something "new" or "different" or "clean" to school every day. I'm just happy as a pig in a prairie wearing my favorite well-fitted T-shirt to school every day!

Want to be like two pigs in a prairie?
You can make your own well-fitted self-portrait T-shirt at home:

You'll need:

A color printer (with ink)

A well-fitted T-shirt of a light color

Iron-on transfer

An iron (Ask an adult for help with the iron. If you're anything like me, you've never used—or seen—one before.)

This here craft is real simple—even for all you printer-unfriendly and ironly inept!

Pretty much, you just need to follow the directions on the iron-on transfer package. Here are some tips:

1. Check the package for directions on figuring out which side of the transfer is the side you print on. When you find it, mark it in the corner so you don't forget.

2. To avoid trouble peeling your transfer off the shirt, be sure to wait for it to set for as long as the directions say. Maybe give your ferret a bath while you wait.

3. Pull the transfer slowly so you can see if it's ready. If it's not, just put the paper back down and iron it more.

4. When you print your transfer, triple check to see whether your printer prints on the top or the bottom, and make sure you line up the side you marked with the side your printer prints on. Try printing a test paper first by putting an X on the front of the paper (face up).

5. After your photo is printed on the transfer, it will look backward. This here ain't a mistake! It's supposed to look backward.

Take a photograph of you wearing your T-shirt, and put it right here!

YOUR PICTURE HERE

6. LUNCH

Lunch is the most important thing on my list. I'm pretty sure if you eat the cafeteria food you will grow an eleventh toe (which isn't entirely bad because having eleven toes sounds awesome!). My point is you don't know what they put in the food at school, so you don't want to take any chances!

Here's my favorite brown-bag lunch: cereal, milk, one serving of fruit and vegetables, a full-length hero sandwich, one lobster, a plate full of tacos, and, naturally, popping rocks. YUMMMM!

Even if your list is complete, you're not ready for school until you also pack your slingshot for gettin' someone's attention, a high-powered car battery for teaching bullies a lesson (Duncanty!), and Mean Girl Repellent for putting that know-it-all Britannica (or any mean girl like her) in her place!

DETENTION

I always say, "Even the well-intentioned get detention!"

On the rare occasion you find yourself in detention (but what really was the big deal about gettin' punched in the face anyway, Duncanty? I mean I hurt my hand too, you know!) . . .

Oops, sorry, I went off-track a bit.

Focus, Terry.

If you find yourself in detention, here are some of my words of wisdom to help get you through it.

Make friends with your fellow detentioners.

That's how I met Fabian (*sigh*), by the way. Before detention, I thought he was just one of those tough kids at school who always got in trouble and got sent to detention. But guess what? He's really super-smart! Truth is, Fabian tries to get in trouble so he'll keep getting detention and hopefully suspended. He values education so much, he never wants to graduate!

Now, there's a role model for ya!

Usually I'm against any form of homework, but if you're stuck in detention, it's the best time to do it.

Actually, some detentions won't let you do homework during detention. Instead they make you sit and stare straight ahead like a zombie for the entire time. So if you're hoping to catch up on your homework in detention so you don't have to do it after school and can work on your carburetor instead, or if you were thinking, "Detention—great! Perfect time to make makeshift papier mâché spitballs and carve my name into the desk!", well, you're gonna have to make a new plan. The detention motto is, "Sit and stare straight ahead," so that's what you should do.

As for me, I'm gonna just keep sittin' here with Fabian (*sigh*) and starin' into space.

BEAUTY IS SKIN DEEP (OR, IMHO, WHAT'S INSIDE IS PRETTIER'N A GLOB A' BUTTER ON A STACK A' WHEAT CAKES!)

Last Mother's Day, when I spent all day at the mall with my buddy Duncanty looking for the perfect gift for my mom for Mother's Day, a light bulb went off in my head.

I said to myself, "Terry, why are you bothering to spend your hard-earned cash on some dumb beauty product when you can make it yourself?"

So Duncanty and me high-tailed it back to my sanctuary, a.k.a. my activity shed, a.k.a. my garage, and whipped up some of the greatest beauty products known to mankind! Er . . . make that ladykind!

Now, even though I believe what counts most in a person is what's on the inside, every now and then even we dirt-lovin' tomboys like to get all dolled up and as flashy as a frog with a gold tooth!

So, presenting my very own Terry the Tomboy line of homemade beauty products you can make yourself, and which won't cost an arm and a leg!

(Well, maybe a frog's leg. How else are you gonna put the green in the green eye shadow?)

MAKEUP

Now don't go running off to buy foundation at the beauty supply store. You can make one that is both cheap and natural right in your own backyard —we're talking about actual *earth* people!

Grab a handful of dirt from your backyard flowerbed, close your eyes for safety purposes, then lightly toss it on your face until it's completely covered. See? It's so natural, it's positively earth-friendly!

Finally, have a good laugh at all those suckers who spent their money at the beauty supply store.

Next, if you're anything like the girls I know, you're gonna want to wear makeup over your foundation. Those girls are not very bright, though. They buy their makeup at expensive stores when all you really need to do is get yourself some good ol' shoe polish! It's very versatile. You can use it as eyeliner and blush!

You're welcome.

PERFUME

Now, personally, I like to smell like myself, not like some flower or tree or rainbow or something. That's why I invented my own signature scent I like to call, "B.Ode to Myself." Here's how you make it.

1. Do a bunch of bench presses while wearing your favorite shirt and get good and sweaty.

2. Ring out the shirt (get as much of your precious perspiration as you can!) and collect the stuff in a spray bottle.

Voila! Not only is my perfume perfect for those days when you're clean as a whistle (ew! I hate those days!), it makes the perfect gift for your mom on Mother's Day! What mother wouldn't want to smell like their child's B.O., am I right?

Don't have time for bench presses? No problem.

1. Rub the tree-shaped air freshener that hangs on your car's rear-view mirror all over yourself.

2. Take a whiff of yourself... you're done!

But if you're one of those people who actually enjoys smelling like a dandelion or a cupcake or a whatever, I suppose you could also make this perfume that I know my cousin Annoying Annie likes to wear. (She's annoying, but she smells pretty good. Most of the time. Anyway, she agreed to give me her recipe, since it was for you guys at home...)

ANNOYING ANNIE'S HOMEMADE PERFUME

You need:

- A clean spray bottle (dark-colored glass works best because it blocks UV rays so your perfume lasts longer)
- A big bottle of pure cooking vanilla—it can't have any sugar in it
- A small bottle of strawberry essential oil (you can get that at the craft store)

Pour the strawberry oil into the spray bottle. Next pour in the vanilla, shake it up…and spray away!

NAILS

I like a good ol' fashioned French manicure as good as the next French girl. But they are *tres* expensive, and who has that kind of cash? Not *moi*!

So what do I do? I use correction fluid!

For just a few bucks a bottle, my French manicure is *tres* mag-*nifique*!

HAIR

Obviously, I take lots of pride in my hair. I also *put* lots of stuff in my hair. No, not fancy hair products. I mean *important* stuff like my wrench.

What good is keeping my wrench at home in my toolbox if I'm at school and a water pipe bursts in the girls' bathroom or something?

C'mon, use your head!

Or, more specifically, your *hair*! If you're like me and want a safe place for keeping all your prized possessions, do what I do: STOP BRUSHING. The knottier and nestier my hair, the better it keeps all my favorite things from falling out!

Genius, I know.

OTHER PRICELESS BEAUTY TIPS FROM TERRY

1. Got bad breath? I carry a big stick with me whenever my breath is particularly rancid. It's perfect for hitting people when they get close enough to smell my breath!

2. Despite what the "experts" tell you, your toenails do *not* have to be trimmed every few weeks. Every few months is more like it! You will, though, need something a little more powerful to cut them with. I use my chain saw…it's perfect!

3. Mom nagging you about your messy hair? Don't pick up that hairbrush. Instead, pick up your favorite hat. Now put it on your head. Presto! Messy hair not a problem!

4. A professional pedicure is really no "cure" for bad feet. Your nasty feet will thank me for this valuable tip: *Manure*. Soak and soften those tootsies in a big, thick pile of cow manure.
(It's the nutrients, I tell ya)

5. Are your teeth whiter and brighter than a polar bear eatin' a trout in the snow? Too-white teeth can burn other people's retinas if they look directly at your mouth. You don't want to be responsible for that, do you? So do what I do, …unwhiten 'em. Here's that time I helped my pal Maddy un whiten her annoyingly bright smile.

6. Zits. Nobody likes 'em, but they don't have to ruin your day. Next time you find one, do what I do: cover the sucker with dirt!

MY MAKEOVER!

Hello, pumpkins! Stop rubbing your eyes. You aren't seeing things—this really is the new me!

I decided to give up that whole tomboy thing, and focus on what really matters: boys and makeup! Welcome to my new channel, Terry's Totally Awesome Fashion Blog!

JUST KIDDING!!!

Do you think I'm NUTS? Why would I ever want to turn all pink and girly-like? I'M JUST PULLIN' YOUR LEG.

Oh, and if you're wondering how my ma reacted to this little prank from last April Fool's Day, she cried real tears of joy! Then we practically had to carry her out of the kitchen on a stretcher when I told her it was just a joke.

Sorry, Ma.

Anyway, if I were to give myself a makeover, it for sure wouldn't be like that. Instead, I'll demonstrate what a true Terry the Tomboy makeover is like, using one of my good friends, Madison.

Now, makin' over Maddy may seem like an impossible task. But it wasn't all that hard. All's I did was change everything about her.

MAKEOVER TIP #1

Maddy's long, wavy hair was so wavy, it was making her seasick. So I ironed it.
Once the stench of burning hair disappeared, and after I teased it a bit with my horse brush, I have to say, it turned out pretty nice.

MAKEOVER TIP #2

"Plaid goes with every eye color," I always say. And this was true for Maddy too, when she finally picked out—with a little persuadin' from yours truly—her new wardrobe. I think she looks AMAZING (a little familiar . . . but AMAZING)!

MAKEOVER TIP #3

A Tomboy's smile is her most important fashion accessory. And I didn't want Maddy's ridiculously bright, white smile to get in the way of her tomboy-ness, so I changed it. As you already know from my "Beauty Is Skin Deep" page earlier, in order to un-whiten Maddy's smile I had to get a *tad* rough with her. But a disclaimer is in order: ****My pal Maddy was not harmed in any way during her BFF Makeover! Except for the little "pinch" she maybe felt after I knocked her tooth out, she was perfectly fine!

MAKEOVER TIP #4

"Stay calm . . . and never leave the house without your lip balm!"

Those, my friends, are words to live by! I make my own lip balm by mixing together a little petroleum jelly for shine and a little shoe polish for color. But if you're uncomfortable wearin' shoe polish on your lips, you can try this recipe I'm pretty sure I once heard Britannica mention.

And it doesn't even taste like potatoes like you might think.

HOMEMADE LIP BALM

You'll need: Petroleum jelly, a packet of a powdered drink mix, a glass bowl, plastic wrap, a microwave, a spoon, and a clean, empty glass container with lid

1. Put some petroleum jelly in a glass bowl and cover with plastic wrap. Melt it in the microwave for 45 seconds.
2. Uncover, and pour in the drink mix. Mix it until all the lumps disappear.
3. Spoon the mixture into the little glass container. DO NOT COVER. Let it set for a while until it cools and stiffens into petroleum jelly again. It's ready!
4. Cover when not using.

THIS HERE'S MY AWESOME STYLE!

Hey there tomcats, tom-toms, and tomboys!

I'm often told I have a great sense of style. And I couldn't agree more! My look is both practical and sturdy, colorful and wordy, and it really screams out to the world, "Terry the Tomboy here!"

The best part of my wardrobe? It's all completely coordinated! Every flannel matches with every T-shirt, which matches with every cap, which goes with everything! Check out these here flannels and tees I made! Which do you like best?

THIS HERE'S MY FAVORITE FLANNEL!

Yup, this here wins for favorite flannel! The best part about this flannel is the material. It's sleeveless, lightweight, and breathable—just perfect for summer! It's also sleeveless, lightweight, and breathable 'cuz I lifted it from my brother Brian's closet and tore off the sleeves. Booty you, Brian!

BULLS-EYE

NO THANKS!

TERRY. KERRY. THE ULTIMATE TOMBOY SHOWDOWN.

I'll never forget the day Kerry moved to town. It was a dark and stormy night. The wind howled through the trees, and there was a foreboding uncertainty in the air.

Well, not really.

But something was definitely up.

The first thing I noticed when I saw Kerry was her hair. It was even more of a mess than mine.

Uh-oh.

And she was chewin' coffee grinds, which is kinda my trademark thing. Or, so I thought. Turned out, she wasn't chewing grinds at all. She was chewing dirt. Straight-up dirt.

I had met my match.

According to section 1.1.1. of the American Tomboy Charter, there can only be one tomboy per school. So there was nothing left to do but grab the fiddles for a good ol' fashioned showdown!

Kerry unleashed the very first hoedown challenge: a spaghetti-eating duel. But she couldn't surpass me—or, should I say surpasta me—as I matched her noodle for noodle, scarfing down as much spaghetti as humanly possible. It was a good effort, Kerry, but you are no match for me when I'm eatin' spaghetti. Or pizza. Or butter, even.

For the showdown's second event, it was my turn to challenge. I knew exactly what I wanted the event to be, so I picked up my trusty slingshot, lined up a few useless dolls, and got busy!

Kerry, though, was up for my challenge. Using her trusty air rifle, she shot all the dolls off the ledge —just like me. Impressive! Even better, when the principal caught Kerry shootin' on school property, he suspended her for a month! At this point in our duel, it looked like it was clear sailing for me!

I let Kerry pick the third, final event. I had to admit, I was mucho impressed with her pick: A Dress-Ruining Competition! Woot-woot! She obviously didn't know who she was dealing with!

Kerry came out of the gate strong, using the ol' "Condiments Catastrophe" technique, and I had to respect her choices, but it was an amateur attempt. I, on the other hand, had a secret weapon up my ugly-blue-taffeta-dress-my-mother-bought-for-me sleeve, and I wasn't afraid to use it: the mud pool.

Valiant attempts from us both, I have to say. And since we couldn't decide on a winner, we just called it a draw and threw out the dumb Tomboy Charter.

And now we're best friends!

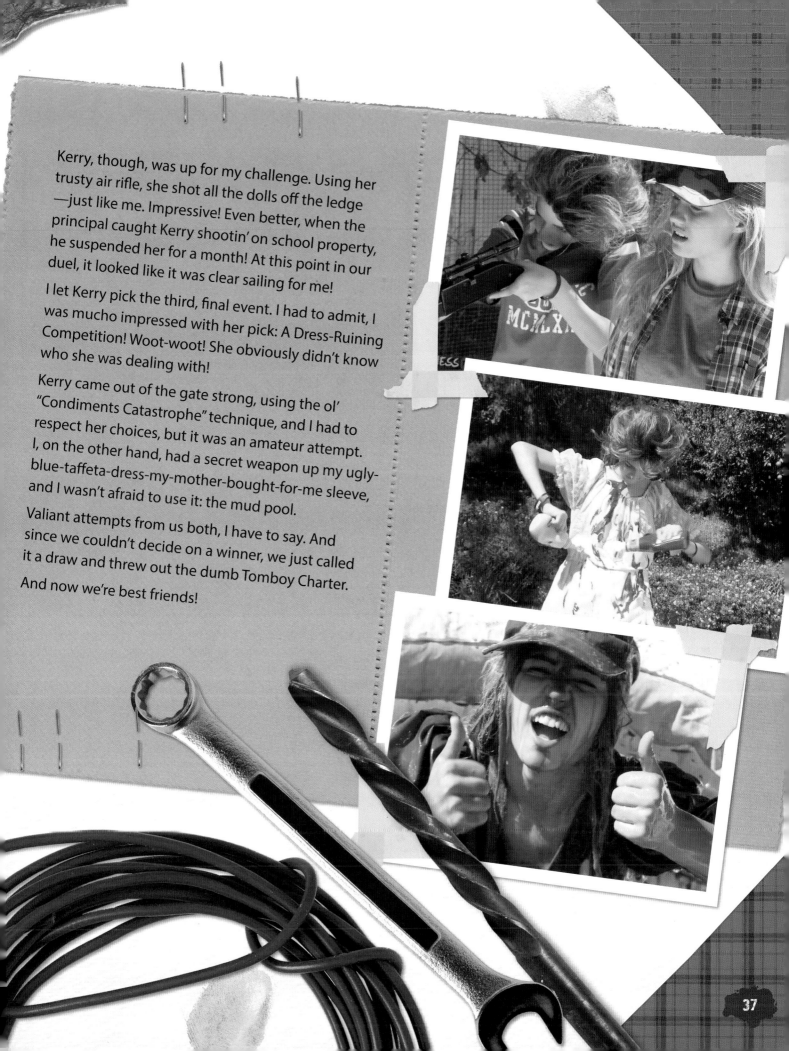

THIS HERE'S MY LOVE LIFE!

(Just kidding—YUCK!—For Real, This Here's My Guide To Dating . . . If You Are Being Forced By Your Ma, That Is!)

Even tomboys go on dates. If you're like me, it's because you are being forced to go by your ma. But sometimes I want to go on a date.

Especially if it means Ma gives me ten bucks for every date I agree to go on! I've made $130 so far, and it's been worth every penny. Sure, I've had to sit through a movie with one of my neighbor's kids, and watch Fourth of July fireworks with some random dude from my math class, but I'm nearly half way to having saved enough money to buy my own ride-on mower!

Anyways, I've learned a lot about dating along the way and thought I'd pass along some of my advice.

1. Once you've spotted the boy of your dreams, it's important to rope him in right away.

2. When I wanted Reese to take me to prom last year, I tricked him into asking. (Genius, no?) I thought up a clever rebus puzzle and had him read it out loud. Sure, it sounded like he was asking me to "pee-ram," but the point is it worked. Next time you want to trick someone into asking you out, try a rebus like this:

Now, if the guy says, "Will sheep go out smell face?", you are crushing on a loser and need to re-examine your love life. But if he's smart, he'll read: Will ewe go out whiff me?—which is good enough.

MOOOO

Again, if you hear, "Lettuce see a cow-vee to moonhouse," you seriously need to rethink your romantic choices. It's "Let us see a movie tonight."

3. Whether you're going out to a movie, having a spittin' contest, or going to a tractor pull (and if it's a tractor pull well you're luckier 'n a dog in a truck with the window down!), you're gonna need transportation. Don't let your date pick your wheels, either. My neighbor's kid picked me up on his bicycle. Seriously. And while not everyone can go driving around in a stylish truck (*sigh*), you can make sure your date has a decent set of wheels.

4. Unfortunately, Terry Hair Hairbrush Hair is frowned upon in social situations. Not by me, personally, but by other folk who care about such things. So if you're headed out in public with your date, you might want to try fixin' up your hair so it will be acceptable to society. Here are some styles to try:

The Beehive Hairdo (made with real honey!)

The British Girl

The Willow

The Former Child Star

The Booty-You To Society, I'm Wearin' My Hair My Way!

5. Don't forget a fragrance for your special night! How about trying a scent that drives guys wild . . . like grease or car oil.

6. When you're on your date, remember to enjoy some friendly competition. Guys love that!

7. If you're going out for a meal, order something not too heavy . . . like ribs.

8. Don't forget your manners. Be ladylike! (This is me on a date belching. It was a good one—long and loud. But I remembered my manners and said "excuse me" in the most ladylike way possible.)

With these Tomboy Dating Tips, you're sure to catch the right guy easier than a bluegill swimmin' upstream!

HOLIDAY TIME!
(A.K.A., A GOOD EXCUSE TO STUFF YOUR FACE!)

I love holidays!

For real, I love every single holiday. In fact, sometimes I make up my own holidays just so I can celebrate somethin'! Bee Appreciation Day? Made that up last summer. Badger Recognition Day? Made that one up, too. And my favorite: Terry's PurgeDay. Why should I celebrate the anniversary of my birth—who cares about that?!? Instead, I like to celebrate the anniversary of the first time I hurled. (November 23, 2006. Right after some bad Thanksgiving pumpkin pie.)

Someday I'm gonna make a separate scrapbook of just holiday celebrations. Until then, I hope y'all will enjoy this whole chapter of my most treasured holiday moments.

CHRISTMAS

A close second to PurgeDay (which is number one only because on PurgeDay I don't have to see my Aunt Millie and Uncle Phillie), Christmas is my favorite holiday. Other than Valentine's Day, when else during the year do I get to use my hatchet? (I'll explain later.)

TREE TRIMMIN' A LA TERRY

Sure, it'd be real easy to get a plastic tree or a tree that's already been cut. But Booty You, Scrooge! In the spirit of Christmas, the right thing to do is to cut down your own tree. That's why, every year, I sneak over to Old Man Finnegan's lot with my hatchet and hack down one of his trees myself!

STEP 1

Once I get my newly cut tree into my work shed, I like to use my chain saw to trim the tree before, well, trimmin' the tree. Plus, it's a good excuse to use my chain saw—a Christmas gift from last year. (Yes, I know what you're thinking . . . Terry, you lucky dog!)

STEP 2

To prevent the pine needles from falling all over the place, you'll need a skirt and a water can to put around the bottom of the tree. I don't have any type of skirt in my work shed—not even a skirt steak—so I just used a Christmas sweater from last year and an old gasoline can.

STEP 3

Tinsel? Booo-riiing!

If you really want to stand out from the crowd, follow my lead and hang bacon strips instead of tinsel on your tree. Your tree will shine with greasy goodness for sure!

Ornaments? Hoooo-huuuummm!

I prefer to use popcorn balls, hand grenades, and—wait for it—meatballs on my tree in place of ornaments! I especially like how the red of the marinara sauce complements the green of my grandpa's old Korean War hand grenades.

STEP 4

You can place a star on top of your tree, but personally I like to use my martial arts throwing stars. This way, I don't have to climb a dangerous ladder to get up there. (I'm all about safety.)

STEP 5

I always say, "every Christmas tree must be lit up more than the year before." So you're gonna need lots and lots of lights for your tree. That can be expensive—and a hassle when they get all tangled up and everything.

I like to use something even better in lieu of lights: SPARKLERS! (A no-brainer, right?) Just look at how pretty they are on my tree! You'll need one of these whenever you want to look at your tree, but so what? It don't get cooler than this!

DON'T GET MIFFED, IT'S MY GUIDE TO GIVING GIFTS

'Tis the season, and you know what that means: you gotta give people stuff.

But luckily, you have me to help you through these confusing times! Look here at some of the great gifts I made all by my lonesome.

SIBLINGS

First, think of what your siblings like. Then think about how you can underhandedly ruin it for them!

For example, my brother Brian is really into fantasy and dragons and stuff. So one year I made him this.

I drew myself as a warrior hero, and if you look closely, you'll see I put Brian in there as well: as my little dwarf sidekick. He was speechless when I gave him this, as you can probably imagine. So I know he loved it!

DADS

Dads really like ties. Sure, you can go brave the spirit-sucking crowds at the mall to buy him a tie from the department store. But why not hang onto your cash and make him a tie instead? If you're like me, you've got tons of dead salamander skins lyin' around. Just stitch 'em together, and you can make your dad an awesome tie like this!

BEFORE

AFTER

MOMS

I don't know about your mom, but you know what my mom always says she wants? She always says she wants me to "clean out that shed of yours—it's too cluttered!"

So that's what I gave her last Christmas! Take a look at these BEFORE and AFTER pictures. Sure, the changes are subtle, but if you look real close, you'll see I finally got rid of my dust mite collection. You're welcome, Mom!

FRIENDS

If your friends are anything like mine, they are always breaking up with their boyfriends or girlfriends and complaining to YOU about it! That's why last Christmas I made my friends the perfect gift: voodoo dolls. Genius, am I right? Now they take out their frustrations on THEM instead!

DUNCANTY

Even if your best friend isn't Duncanty, you'll want to get him or her the most perfect gift ever. In my humble opinion, that most perfect gift ever is a pet! Last Christmas I gave Duncanty my precious pet squirrel, Bedford. Unfortunately, he let Bedford get away when he carelessly and recklessly opened the box and I really let him have it, but I think he still appreciated the sentiment.

Hope you got some good ideas for holiday gift giving from my experiences! Have a Merry Christmas, video blog friends, and remember: avoid the mall at all costs!

THANKSGIVING

Every November (October for y'all in Canada) we think of things we're thankful for. What a bore.

Here are all the reasons why I love Turkey Day:

• It's an excuse to stuff your face!

• I love me some turkey!

• I get to hunt for my own turkey with my authentic Plains Indian turkey hatchet!

• I get to help my mom make pumpkin pie! (No canned pumpkin at the Ptarmigan household! No, sir-eee!)

• Eating a ton is encouraged!

• I get to make my world-famous sweet potatoes, just like the pilgrims made! (Simple recipe, really. Just take regular french fries and mix 'em with something sweet like sugar or honey. Oh, and if you want your 'taters to look authentic, just mix in some cheese puffs!)

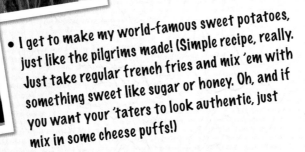

43

VALENTINE'S DAY

Before you say, "Valentine's Day, Terry? You like Valentine's Day?", you should know I DO like Valentine's Day because of the satisfaction I get in helpin' others fall madly and deeply in love. *Sigh*

And if you believe that, I've got a genuine golden goose to sell you. (I do own a golden goose—her name's Miranda —but she's not golden 'cuz she's made a' gold. She's golden 'cuz I spilled glitter gold nail polish on her feathers tryin' to give her bill a real sparkle when I entered her in the state fair. My bad, Miranda!)

Anywho . . . If you're looking to win over your date this February 14, you'd be smarter 'n a catnip-sellin' Siamese if you follow my Terry The Tomboy Guide To Valentine's Day!

HOW TO WIN OVER YOUR DATE

Give her your heart.

Well, not your real heart, silly! Of course I mean a cow's heart. She'll love the romantic gesture!

Tell her how you feel with candy hearts.

If you're anything like me, you hate those sappy sayings written on candy hearts. So do what I do, and make your own! It's easy! First, suck off all the sappy sayings on the candy that comes in the box. Next, think of something real romantic you want to say to her. Something short and simple, like:

HEY I THINK YOU'RE REALLY GREAT MAYBE WE COULD GO HANG OUT SOMETIME AND YA KNOW HANG OUT BY THE CREEK OR THUMB WRESTLE OR SOMETHING

After you've picked a romantic message, it's time to write it on the candy heart with a toothpick and some red food coloring.

    Voila!

HEY I THINK YOU'RE REALLY GREAT MAYBE WE COULD GO HANG OUT SOMETIME AND YA KNOW HANG OUT BY THE CREEK OR THUMB WRESTLE OR SOMETHING

NEW YEAR'S EVE

Wanna throw the best fest in the west? Well, sit down class and don't be tardy. It's my Guide To The Perfect New Year's Party!

My brother Brian took these pictures of me gettin' ready for my big New Year's Eve bash a few years ago. And it's a good thing he did, too; otherwise, I wouldn't have these great photos to go along with my Guide To The Perfect New Year's Party!

TIP #1

Make your invitations by hand.

Here's the one I made for Duncanty. Hahahaha . . . oh, Duncanty! Sometimes I just can't help myself from messin' with you. I promise—no more pranks until next year! (Think he'll realize "next year" is just hours away?)

TIP #2

Forget the balloons—balloons are old news. Instead, blow up a hundred or so surgical gloves!

They look way cool and, as an extra added bonus, your guests will have something to high five at those awkward moments when they're looking for someone to high five and are left hangin'!

TIP #3

Have a jerky variety.

Obviously, you're gonna want to serve your guests an assortment of different flavored jerkys. Reindeer flavored is, of course, my favorite for the holidays. A bit gamey at first, but flavorful nonetheless.

TIP #4

Combine serving beverages with party games.

That time I lost the top to my blender, I had the greatest idea ever: What better than to make a party game out of blending the eggnog?

Add your ingredients to the blender, then gather your friends around with their glasses. Turn on the blender. Whoever gets the most 'nog in their glass . . . wins the most 'nog!

TIP #5

Save a duck.

Being prepared with suitable noisemakers for the arrival of midnight is a key component of a good New Year's Eve party.

My personal preference would be to give a duck from my backyard pond to all my party guests. Then, when the clock strikes midnight, have everyone give their little duckling a squeeze!

But I can see where some people might not be comfortable with squeezing a duck. And, I guess, the ducks might not enjoy gettin' squeezed either.

So I came up with a way you can make homemade noisemakers, and no ducklings will be harmed in the process.

Plastic Straw Duck Call

1. Flatten one end of a drinking straw by pressing down on it with your finger.

2. Next, cut the flattened end to make a triangular tip.

3. Finally, put the triangular end into your mouth and blow.

QUACK, QUACK! HAPPY NEW YEAR!

BIRTHDAYS ... PURGEDAYS ... CHRISTMASES ... BADGER RECOGNITION DAYS.

Whenever there's a gift-givin' holiday, I'm three pounds a lucky stuffed in a two-pound sack because it always means a NEW CAP for me! Here are some of my all-time favorite caps. Hope you enjoy looking at 'em as much as I enjoy wearing 'em!

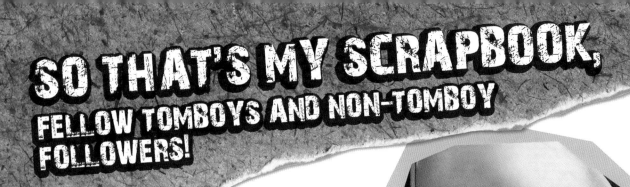

SO THAT'S MY SCRAPBOOK,
FELLOW TOMBOYS AND NON-TOMBOY FOLLOWERS!

Hope you liked my photos— I've had more fun than a squirrel in a nut patch sharing them with y'all!

Bye for now, and remember:

A LITTLE GRIME IS MORE THAN FINE!

See ya next time!